POPEYE
THE FIRST FIFTY YEARS

POPEYE

THE FIRST FIFTY YEARS

by Bud Sagendorf

Workman Publishing

King Features Syndicate
New York

To Nadia, who was also there

For their valuable help, thanks to
Bradley Sagendorf, Marie Segar
Clausen, Nadia Sagendorf, Theda and
Frank Ripperdan and all the wonderful
people of Chester, Illinois.

Copyright © 1979 by King Features Syndicate,
Inc. and Workman Publishing Company, Inc.

Library of Congress Cataloging in
Publication Data

Sagendorf, Bud.
Popeye, the first fifty years.

1. Thimble theatre [Comedy strip] I. Title
PN6728.T5S2   741.5'973   78-65820
ISBN 0-89480-066-3
ISBN 0-89480-065-5 pbk.

Jacket and book design: Paul Hanson

Workman Publishing Company, Inc.
1 West 39 Street
New York, New York 10018

Manufactured in the United States of America
First printing May 1979
10   9   8   7   6   5   4   3   2   1

CONTENTS

PAGE 69

FOREWORD

Since his first appearance fifty years ago, Popeye has exerted a tremendous influence on the comic-reading public. Elzie Crisler Segar's THIMBLE THEATRE was a new kind of daily continuity comic strip, and influenced many aspiring young cartoonists who dreamed of someday creating a comic strip of their own. As one of these ambitious dreamers, it was my good fortune to become Segar's first and only assistant—and at a peak time, since Popeye had been in the strip just a little over a year.

As most cartoonists do, Segar worked at home. I was underfoot night and day in the Segar home, and would have to be accepted by Mrs. Segar and the Segar children, Marie and Tommy. I will always be grateful to those wonderful people who allowed me in their home and made me feel a member of the family.

Segar was a fun boss as well as a kind and patient teacher. Even when deadlines were tight, there was always time to explain to his green assistant how and why he was doing a particular thing in the writing or drawing.

These were the most creative and productive years of Segar's work, and to be there and participate in a small way in the creation of such wonderful characters as the Jeep, Swee'pea, Pappy, the Goon, etc., was an education and experience few young cartoonists have the chance to share.

If, when reading about these simple but extraordinary cartoon characters, the reader becomes aware of a tendency to think of them as real people, expect no apologies from the author—they *are* real people. My family and I have lived with them day and night for most of our lives. Their problems have been our problems, and at times, ours have been theirs.

And, YES, we *do* eat our spinach!

Bud Sagendorf

SETTING THE STAGE

Elzie Crisler Segar (1894-1938)

SEGAR'S EARLY YEARS

Like that other great teller of stories, Elzie Crisler Segar was born in a small town on the banks of the muddy Mississippi. Chester, Illinois, has grown through the years, and so has the town's pride in its illustrious son. This pride has culminated in the creation of Segar Memorial Park. Located on a bluff overlooking the Mississippi, the park has as its focal point a six-foot bronze statue of the fat-armed sailor. Popeye, on his marble pedestal, has only to look over his left shoulder and down the bluff to see the house where his creator spent many nights at work on his cartoon-art correspondence course, dreaming of becoming a big-time cartoonist.

Young Segar's childhood closely followed the Tom Sawyer pattern of swimming, fishing and rafting on the great river. There was even an island where the boy and his pals could play. His love of fishing was to stay with him all his life. Later on, much of his creative work was done in a rowboat or on a pier with pole in hand. Walter Berndt, of SMITTY fame, recalls their early years together in New York City: "Segar and I would sneak out of the office, go over to New Jersey and spend the afternoon fishing from a dilapidated pier. We'd talk over ideas and would come home with a big bag of fish and about twenty ideas each."

The modest means of his family sparked in the youthful Segar a desire and knack for making money. In later years, he made no bones about the fact that his chosen field was linked directly to reading about the huge salaries made by better-known cartoonists. His ingenuity for moneymaking is illustrated by the visit of a U.S. navy ship to Chester, whose residents flocked to the river to be ferried out to the vessel for twenty-five cents each. Several days before, ten-year-old Segar had found an old rowboat with a large hole in its side. Realizing the fortune to be made, he patched the boat, and from the cove above the town dock he did a booming business rowing local boys and girls to the warship for only five cents apiece.

At twelve, Elzie Segar began his first steady employment. He went to work at the Chester Opera House, the local cultural center and silent-movie house, and earned what to him must have been a huge sum—fifty cents a day. He was in charge of changing weekly posters around town, drawing show bills for the front of the theater, creating advertising slides to be used while reels were being changed and playing drums to accompany Jessie Lee Huffstutler's piano. Saturday mornings, he arrived early at the opera house and with colored chalks drew cartoons on the sidewalk to advertise the week's movie. Even with these many chores, he found time to become a full-fledged motion-picture projectionist. He was so proud of this accomplishment that he had M.P.O. tattooed on his arm—for Motion Picture Operator.

Elzie Crisler Segar Memorial Park, Chester, Illinois, dedicated June 25, 1977. The six-foot bronze statue of the *famous sailor, sculpted by Robert L. Walker, attracts visitors to Segar's birthplace.*

In his off-hours, he was a house painter, paper hanger and window dresser. His first true art job was the talk of the town. A local hardware merchant wanted an eye-catching billboard painted on the side of a barn, and Segar was commissioned to do the work for twenty-five dollars. Several gallons of paint later, and after many hours atop a shaky ladder, the job was finished. The entire town turned out to see the finished product, and the boy was congratulated for his masterpiece. A great future was assured the budding artist—until it rained a week later. The inexperienced Michelangelo had used a water-based paint, and the masterpiece dissolved into puddles of colored water at the base of the barn. Segar later said, "They were very pretty puddles, but you couldn't read 'em."

The opera house owner, Bill Schuchert, encouraged Segar in his cartooning, and with this and the praise he'd received from town folks, he decided it was time to spread his talent out to a waiting world. His first submission of drawings was mailed to a St. Louis newspaper with the note: "Please publish my cartoons on account of I have an uncle working in your press room." The uncle either had little influence or wasn't consulted by the editor; the drawings were returned.

With rejection, Elzie Segar grew more determined and sent for the Evans Correspondence Course in Cartooning. Bill Schuchert paid the twenty dollars for the course because he felt, even if St. Louis didn't, that his young employee had a future as a cartoonist. After eighteen months of study and hundreds of drawings, Segar finished the course. He later said he got Schuchert's money's worth: when the lesson called for one drawing, he'd send eight or ten, and Mr. Evans would criticize all of them without complaint. Several months later, he packed his bag with pens, pencils and paper, and wearing the only clothes he owned, he left for Chicago.

SEGAR
IN CHICAGO

Segar's first challenge in Chicago was to locate his half-brother, whom he finally contacted after a helpful stranger told him people were looked up in the phone book by *last* names, not first. Shortly thereafter, he was introduced by his brother to R. F. Outcault, creator of the BUSTER BROWN cartoon. Outcault sent him to the Chicago *Herald*, where the editor asked if he were really a cartoonist. Segar replied he certainly was—after all, he had a fancy diploma from Mr. Evans saying so—and if they were smart they'd hire him. He was assigned to writing and drawing a comic strip called CHARLIE CHAPLIN'S COMIC CAPERS, a well-known feature that had been drawn by many men through the years and had proven valuable work for the beginning cartoonist to cut his teeth on. Segar's correspondence course had trained him strictly in editorial cartooning, with no comic-strip lessons, but he threw himself into the job. Also, during this period, he married Myrtle Johnson of Chicago.

When the *Herald* folded, Segar quickly located himself with the Chicago *American*, where he created a feature titled LOOPING THE LOOP. More an illustrated column than a comic strip, the feature called for a daily review of theaters, nightclub acts and any special events taking place in Chicago. At this point in his career, Segar had to make a decision. The feature had proven successful, and his editor suggested there would be a lot more room for words in his column if he'd stop putting in those silly little drawings.

Luckily, his drawing and humor had caught the eye of Arthur Brisbane, a great newspaper man of the Hearst organization, and he was offered a job in New York City with King Features Syndicate. Segar didn't want to be trapped forever into writing a column, and he jumped at the chance to continue his dream of becoming a big-time cartoonist. Soon he was on his way to the big city and THIMBLE THEATRE.

One of the last LOOPING THE LOOP cartoon columns

SEGAR CREATES THIMBLE THEATRE

Arriving in New York City, the eager young cartoonist was told to create a comic strip based on the title THIMBLE THEATRE. This was an especially exciting period of expansion in comic art—the infant comic strip was finally growing up, and comics were recognized as circulation builders by editors and publishers.

William Randolph Hearst, as a test, had ordered his editors at a Midwestern paper to switch BRINGING UP FATHER from the morning paper to the afternoon edition. In two days, the morning paper lost thousands of readers—while the afternoon edition picked up an equal number. The test proved that the American public loved comics and didn't want to miss a single day in the adventures of their favorites. The fun of drawing comic pictures of a teacher in a school notebook had become big business.

No longer did individual newspapers hire artists to draw comic strips exclusively for their paper: syndication had been perfected. In partnership with the syndicates, cartoonists had their features appearing in hundreds of papers, foreign and domestic—an arrangement that not only allowed millions of newspaper readers to be exposed to and love comics, but also increased the earnings of the comic artist. Newspapers pay for nonsalaried, contract comic artists on the basis of the individual paper's circulation. This price is, and was, from a few dollars a week for small circulation dailies to much more for large city papers. The earnings are split between syndicates and cartoonist-writers. The more papers sold, the larger the profits are for both.

New York has always been the mecca of young, aspiring cartoonists. And it was especially so for Elzie and Myrtle Segar when they arrived several days before he was to begin work at King Features. After paying a week's room rent, their money was more than limited, and the couple decided they should spend what was left on a suit for Elzie. He didn't want to show up at his new job looking like a country rube. The Segars found a small basement men's shop with huge signs advertising SUITS—BARGAINS! and with much care they chose a conservative, light tan suit. The shopkeeper promised the alterations would be finished early Monday morning, the day Elzie was to report to work.

At the appointed time, Segar picked up the boxed suit and hurried back to their room to put it on. To his horror, the suit was not the color it seemed in the dimness of the men's shop. Instead, in the daylight, it was almost bright orange. There was neither the time nor the money to do anything about the clothing, and as Segar would later remark, "I was dressed like a short, thin pumpkin whose light had gone out."

The cartoonist was in for another

They are hard to recognize

But they are Ham Gravy, Olive Oyl and brother Castor

surprise when he arrived at his office. There was no space in the Hearst newspaper building for the comic art department, so a room in the building next-door was leased for its use. The two buildings were about ten feet apart, and rather than take the elevators down and up, the cartoonists had placed a narrow plank between the fourth-floor windows of the buildings. Segar later said the plank forever destroyed his illusions about slick sophistication in the big city. He never got used to crawling between buildings, four floors up, above hard concrete.

In this wonderful period of change, and almost overnight, Segar created the Oyl family—with the addition of Ham Gravy for love interest. THIMBLE THEATRE was underway.

The title of the feature was a lucky break for Segar—it gave him the opportunity to let his imagination run rampant with the stories as well as the characters. Had he been told to name the strip for one of its principals—Olive Oyl, Castor Oyl or Ham Gravy—this freedom would not have been possible. He would have been unable to make a permanent place in the cast for Wimpy,

Eugene the Jeep, Alice the Goon and Popeye.

The new comic started as a gag-a-day feature—each day complete unto itself. As time went by, however, the daily strip was more and more based on a theme lasting a week or more. During a conversation with Segar at a roadside diner, I asked how and why he had turned to continuity, he told me he was never consciously aware he was doing it—he just liked to tell stories. The idea of Castor Oyl and Ham Gravy going to Dice Island (1929) called for a continued story, and with the addition of Popeye at this time a story theme was well established. Sailors have adventures, and adventures call for long stories.

Segar had used continued stories in pre-Popeye Sunday pages, and several times he tried to use them during the thirties. Each time, he was ordered to stop. Newspaper editors didn't approve—the individual Sunday gags with Popeye, Wimpy and Geezil were too popular to be diluted. Finally, the popularity of continued stories in daily form proved overwhelmingly successful.

THIMBLE THEATRE—THE ORIGINAL CAST

OLIVE

HAM GRAVY
(Olive's first boy friend)

COLE OYL
(Olive's father)

NANA OYL
(Olive's mother)

CASTOR OYL
(Olive's brother)

TWO GREAT INFLUENCES

The work of all creative people is influenced by those they admire, and Segar could not have selected two men of more genius than Charlie Chaplin and George Herriman.

As a young projectionist in Illinois, Segar had many opportunities to study the films of Chaplin, and it is clear that many of the elements in the pre-Popeye THIMBLE THEATRE were reminiscent of the little tramp's one- and two-reel comedies. Chaplin's *Easy Street*, for example, featured many of the staples found in Segar's early strips: the huge villain with rough, black beard and mustache, the little hero—and, of course, the maiden in distress.

And, along with many other cartoonists, Segar felt the influence of George Herriman's humor and his ability to paint with a pen. Little touches of Herriman's style continually showed up in the backgrounds and figures of THIMBLE THEATRE.

Shortly before Herriman's death in the forties, Mrs. Sagendorf and I had the opportunity to spend an afternoon with this great man. Driving up a narrow road to the top of one of the Hollywood Hills, we came to a rambling home perched on the edge of a cliff. It had to be Herriman's home. It looked as though he had drawn it there—the brick wall, the brilliant house trim, and the potted plants were right out of KRAZY KAT.

During the entire visit, Herriman discussed nothing but Segar—his work and his humor. It was apparent that his respect for the cartoonist matched Segar's admiration of him.

Segar and Herriman were shy, quiet men who even looked alike, and they both had strong feelings of privacy. It is not surprising, therefore, that the two giants of their profession lived for over twenty years within eighteen miles of each other and never met. Because of their mutual awe, neither felt he had the right to impose on the other.

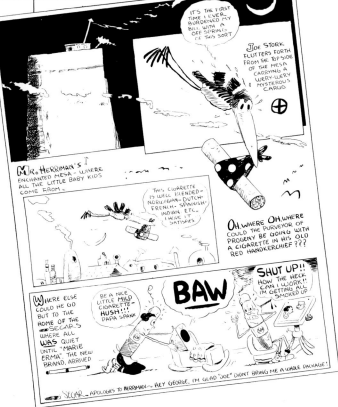

A rare STUMBLE INN daily strip from 1922—Herriman's human figures had a great influence on Segar's early style

Segar's admiration for George Herriman is shown in the birth announcement telling of the arrival of the Segar's first child, Marie Erma Segar, in 1922; this drawing appeared in the Hearst organization's magazine, Circulation

19

POPEYE ENTERS THIMBLE THEATRE, JANUARY 17, 1929

When Castor Oyl and Ham Gravy gained possession of Bernice the Whiffle Hen, they thought their future was secure. They had discovered Bernice was a "lucky hen," and they were determined to use this knowledge to their financial advantage. The plan was to take the hen to Mr. Fadewell's gambling casino on Dice Island. With their mascot, they couldn't lose at any game of chance.

For six thousand dollars, the would-be sports purchased a splendid sailing ship for their voyage to wealth. The vessel was a real buy: as Castor told Ham Gravy, she had only a few holes in her hull—luckily, all below the waterline, where they wouldn't show.

With provisions aboard—one thousand cans of beans, three dill pickles and one bar of soap—the two men were ready to sail when they realized neither had the slightest knowledge of how to "drive a boat." They would have to find an experienced sailor to see them safely to Dice Island and the gaming tables.

As logical adventurers would, they searched the waterfront. Seafaring jobs must have been plentiful, for they found only one man in need of employment—a strange-looking character with a jutting chin and one eye. After assuring himself that this odd figure was indeed a sailor, Castor hired him on the spot.

Readers of THIMBLE THEATRE that day could not know they had witnessed the birth of a legend and folk hero.

Many of the citizens of Chester, Illinois, Segar's hometown, are convinced that his famous sailor was inspired by a local character named Rocky Feigle. Rocky, a thin, wiry man, was employed part-time to sweep and clean up in the local saloon. His afternoons were spent leaning back in a chair in front of his place of work. Known as the town's cock of the walk, Rocky was famous for never having lost a fight, and it was a challenge for small boys—Segar included—to tease him with the hope he would give chase. On one occasion, three local toughs lured Rocky out into the woods, where they planned to rob him. A short time later, Rocky, in true Popeye style, nonchalantly strolled back into town and resumed his customary seat in front of the saloon. Meanwhile, the three would-be muggers sought medical aid for injuries received in their robbery attempt.

Frank "Rocky" Feigle of Chester, Illinois

SEGAR: JANUARY 17, 1929

Ask a stupid question …

And you'll get one back

It is also a common belief in Chester that Rocky Feigle, in his later years, received a weekly check from Popeye's creator.

Whether these beliefs are fact or fiction, Popeye was waiting backstage for the opportunity to step into the limelight.

WHIFFLE!

Three hairs–rub them and they bring luck

Bernice the Whiffle Hen was certainly a "lucky hen" for Segar and THIMBLE THEATRE, but not for Castor Oyl and Ham Gravy. True, they made a fortune on Dice Island, but they paid a tremendous price. Popeye, the sailor they hired, would soon outshine them.

SEGAR: JANUARY 24, 1929

POPEYE FINDS OLIVE

When Olive first heard about the plans to sail to Dice Island, she took it for granted that she'd be included. After all, she was Castor's sister, and Ham Gravy was her boyfriend. To her disgust, she was told: "Only men go down to the sea in ships." Resenting this chauvinistic attitude—and picturing Ham Gravy with "tropical dames under a moon as big as a house"—Olive grew determined to take part in the venture.

To rid themselves of the pesky girl at sailing time, the two men sent her off to buy "a dime's worth of longitude." While she was being directed from store to store by snickering merchants, Castor and Ham Gravy set sail. But the new hired hand had forgotten to hoist the anchor, and lucky Olive found plenty of time to sneak aboard and stow away in the sail locker.

Her presence wasn't discovered till the ship and crew were far from harbor and on the high seas. Popeye, the new member of the cast, came upon the stowaway in the hold of the ship and brought her to the attention of Captain Castor.

Popeye had no time for the unwelcome passenger—stowaways were criminals and had to be punished. Put to work washing dishes in the galley, Olive in turn had nothing but contempt for the crude sailor who carried out her brother's orders.

The first meeting of the future lovers, on January 24, 1929, was a most unromantic happening. As with many famous couples, it gave no hint of the relationship to come. One thing is sure—it wasn't love at first sight.

Olive wasn't impressed with her future sweety

SEGAR: JANUARY 25, 1929

POPEYE'S HOMETOWN

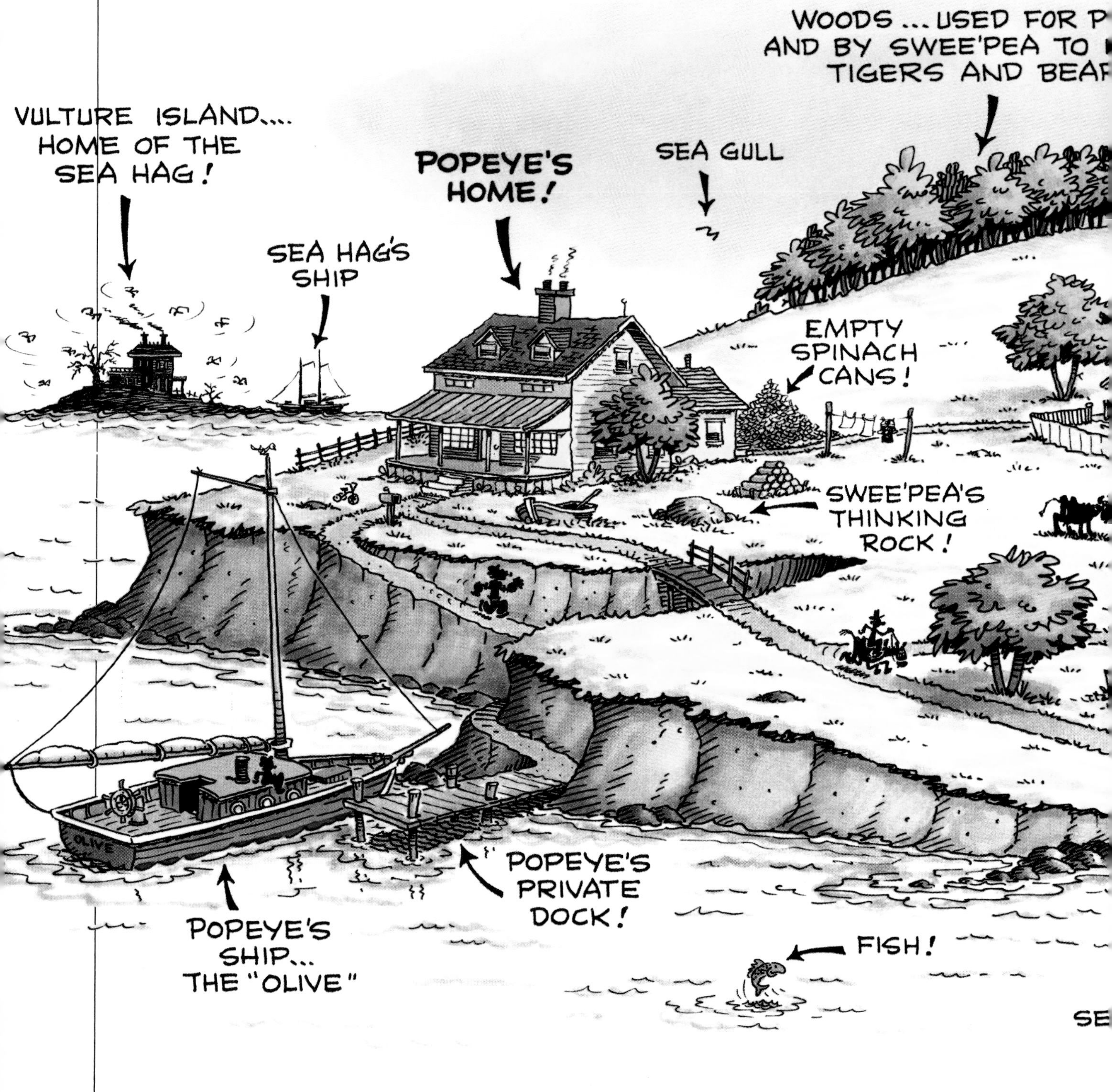

VULTURE ISLAND....
HOME OF THE
SEA HAG!

SEA HAG'S
SHIP

POPEYE'S
HOME!

SEA GULL

WOODS ...USED FOR P
AND BY SWEE'PEA TO
TIGERS AND BEAR

EMPTY
SPINACH
CANS!

SWEE'PEA'S
THINKING
ROCK!

POPEYE'S
PRIVATE
DOCK!

POPEYE'S
SHIP...
THE "OLIVE"

FISH!

SE

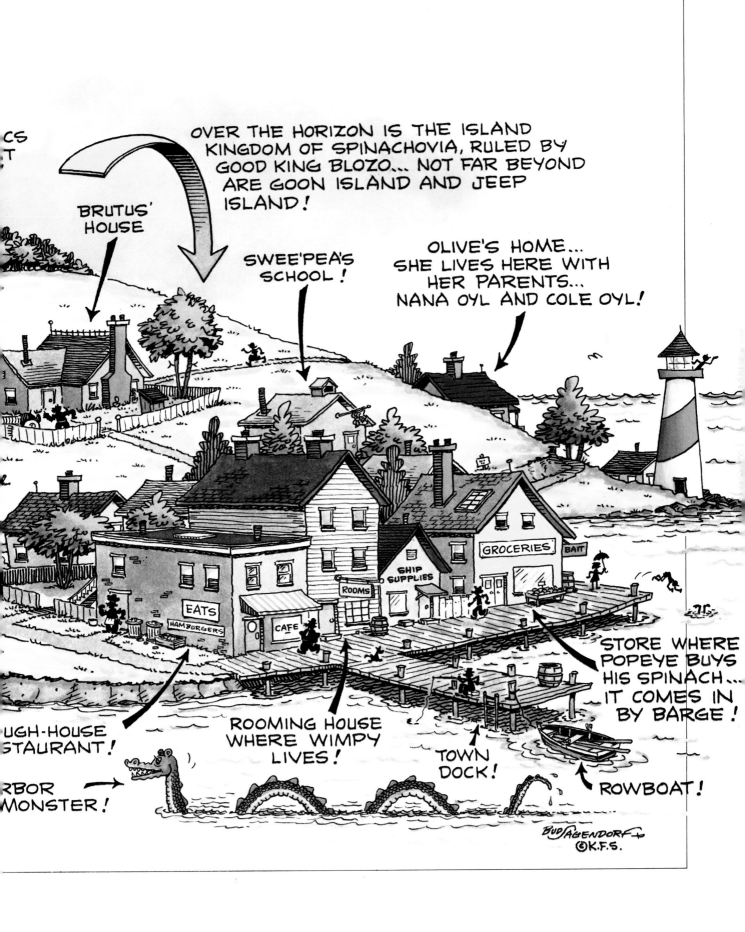

The future SAPPO *top piece is born as* THE FIVE-FIFTEEN *daily strip*

SEGAR: DECEMBER 20, 1921

THE FIVE-FIFTEEN

Walter Berndt, creator of the unique SMITTY comic strip, has described how Segar came to introduce the well-known FIVE-FIFTEEN feature. Though Segar grew up along the Mississippi and Berndt was born in Brooklyn, they were both avid fishermen. Several days a week, the two cartoonists sneaked out of their offices and took the ferry to New Jersey, where they fished along the Hudson River.

King Features' comic art director at the time became aware that one of his flock (the cartoonists all sat together in a large room under his eagle eye) was rushing through his work and then playing hooky. Undoubtedly a man who preferred poker and golf to angling, he took Segar to task—if there was time to waste on fishing, there was time to produce yet another comic strip for the company. THE FIVE-FIFTEEN was thus forced onto the pages of American newspapers.

The feature debuted in 1921, centered on a short character named John Sappo and his large wife Myrtle (named after Segar's own wife). It was a gag-a-day strip about the suburbs and the commuter's way of life.

For several years, FIVE-FIFTEEN flourished in its original format. Then, in the late twenties, Segar redesigned the strip. It was customary at this time for newspapers to divide the Sunday comics page into two sections—the main feature taking up about three-fourths of the lower portion, another feature by the same cartoonist occupying the top. When Segar needed to create a "top piece" for his THIMBLE THEATRE Sunday page, he converted SAPPO and added a character named Professor O. G. Watasnozzle, a brilliant scientist and mad inventor.

Segar had always loved science fiction, using it frequently even in pre-Popeye THIMBLE THEATRE strips. But with Sappo and Watasnozzle at his command, he moved full force into the world of the future. Watasnozzle, in the early thirties, was splitting atoms as easily as walnuts. Sappo and the professor visited distant planets with ease. Whenever the spirit moved them to travel, Segar simply inked them a spaceship and off they went.

John and Myrtle Sappo

When the first walks in space astonished the world, Sappo and Watasnozzle only yawned. It was old hat to them—Sappo's wife Myrtle had space-walked in 1937.

In the real world, Segar was an inventive amateur engineer. A master with tools, he designed much of the equipment used in his photography studio. One of his creations was a camera and enlarger to reproduce thousands of special drawings to mail to fans who wrote him. Though it looked like a project from O. G. Watasnozzle's mind, it worked flawlessly. As his assistant, it was my job to operate the machine. There was only one minor problem—Segar's favorite building material was wood yardsticks, and when operating the camera it was sometimes difficult to tell which of the many scales to use.

A 1937 walk in space

SEGAR: JULY 18, 1937

The THIMBLE THEATRE top piece

SEGAR: NOVEMBER 28, 1937

Professor O.G. Watasnozzle
"The Atomic Brain"

SEGAR AT WORK

Short of stature, slight of frame, mild-mannered and somewhat introverted, Segar was the complete opposite of his spinach-eating creation—with one exception. For a small man, his strength was phenomenal. As his assistant, I would be given a job requiring muscles, and many times I had to ask for his help. Maybe I wasn't eating enough spinach.

In his few social activities, he was reserved and uncomfortable—especially with people he didn't know. Many times, when large functions were planned, he would make what to him was the logical excuse that we were going fishing to work on an idea. An excellent billiards player, he had played many of the top professionals and for an "amateur" had won more than his share of the matches. Like most boys growing up in small towns, he had spent much of his spare time in the only available recreation establishment—the pool hall. His dream was to make enough money to afford billiard tables of his own. When the Segars built their home in Santa Monica, California, a room was constructed off the studio just for the pool and billiard tables.

After New York City, a very short stay in Florida and a few years in Hollywood, Santa Monica was finally selected as a permanent homesite. The location was chosen for its pleasant surroundings, but I have always thought its proximity to the ocean and its fine

Segar working at home

fishing pier were the reasons. Segar had three loves: his family, his work and fishing. He didn't care for sport fishing, as such, and didn't go after the big ones. He liked to eat what he caught, so nearly all his angling from the pier was for pan fish. Between the ages of eight and twelve, I haunted the same pier, fished with a drop line and mooched bait from fellow fishermen. Segar and I wondered how many times we had stood side by side, fishing.

Segar was a night worker, and this meant his assistant was, too. Our usual hours were from seven or eight at night till four or five in the morning. This was tough on a high school student. It wasn't that I worried about my school work; it was that I didn't have the time to pursue the girl I had chosen to be my wife. Fortunately, Segar was most understanding, and between pages or strips I was allowed to dash off for a date with the young lady. Few mothers would understand a boy picking up her daughter at three in the morning for a fast hamburger.

At least once a week, usually on my night off, Segar would call around midnight to tell me it was time to work on ideas. This meant I was to call the pier, have the boat put in the water, gather the fishing gear and pick him up. Much of the basic, creative thinking was done in this boat, tied to what was then the new Santa Monica breakwater. With fishhooks baited and lines in the water, we would settle down to discuss the next week's work. I always had a pad illuminated by a gasoline lantern to make notes.

A great part of creating humor is getting into the mood. The more outlandish and bizarre the ideas, the better. When the point is reached where you're laughing at anything, you can settle down to the selection of workable segments. During these warmups, we'd explode into wild bursts of laughter. People trying to sleep on nearby boats must have thought there was a drunken brawl going on. If they yelled and cursed at us, we never knew it; we were too involved to notice. Of course, when either of us hooked a fish, the laughter would cease—pulling in a fish is serious business and no time for levity.

In the mid-thirties, Segar discovered there was a skeet club in Santa Monica. If fishing was his first love as a sport, shooting was the second. In a short time, he was a member of the club, and a new life style evolved. An excellent shot, he was soon club champion and captain of the skeet team. Suddenly, the boy from the small river town in Illinois found himself in the company—and a teammate— of Eugene Pallette, Clark Gable and Gary Cooper. Segar and Pallette became good friends and spent many afternoons, with me as an awed observer, teaching "The King" the fine art of bird shooting. Most of these men belonged to a duck club up the coast at Oxnard. Eugene Pallette had a cabin there, and Segar was easily convinced it would be a nice place for his family and a quiet place for us to work. So a cabin was built (they called them cabins, but they were really very comfortable homes). In several Popeye Sunday pages, there are references to the Santa Monica Rod and Reel Club, and many ideas came from the hours spent here and at the skeet club.

In the mid-twenties, Segar had a great desire to paint and one day struck up an acquaintance with a man sketching on the pier. The result of this meeting was: if Segar would lease a studio and equip it with painting materials, the man would give him lessons. An office was quickly rented in a new downtown building at Fourth and Broadway in Santa Monica. The lessons lasted only a few months—Segar had learned all the painter had to offer. The office was kept for work, and the painter went on to oblivion.

This was the office where Popeye was born in 1929. On the day he would draw the first rough sketch of the sailor, Segar was sick with a bad cold. Mrs. Segar begged him to stay home, but at the last minute he decided to see if he could at least get a start on that week's set of dailies. Off he went—to what was his most important day's work. In later years, he often wondered whether he ever would have created Popeye if he had not gone to the office that day. Knowing his working methods and day-to-day inspirations, it is doubtful he would have thought of this particular sailor at a later time—it might be a different sailor who won the love of Olive.

One morning at the duck club, Segar and I were eating dinner and watching the sun come up when he began to reminisce about those days in the office where he created Popeye. He told about a funny little kid who had sold him his evening papers. This small boy in overalls would be waiting for him, rain or shine, each evening. Segar stopped speaking when he saw the startled expression on my face. He asked me what was wrong, and I said, "Nothing." But I asked him a few questions, and sure enough: *I* was that paper boy. It was my first job, and where I was assigned to sell my papers was the least choice corner in the city. I stuck it out because I had one steady customer, a kind man who'd give me a nickel or a dime for a three-cent copy of the Los Angeles *Herald-Express* and never wait for change. Of course, I didn't realize my steady customer drew THIMBLE THEATRE, the comic strip, that ran in

Segar photographing a cartoon much like this one which he presented to me on our first meeting

the paper he bought from me day after day.

Though Segar was uncomfortable at social events, he was always at home seated at a lunch counter, drugstore or roadside diner. He was at ease with everyday people and never hesitated to start a conversation with the man next to him. He did have one pet peeve. The question of occupation would come up, and after the stranger's business was discussed, Segar would be asked about his work. When he answered that he wrote and drew a comic strip, the stranger would invariably laugh and say, "That's great, but what do you do for a living?" Segar would boil inside, his face would turn red, and I'd know it was time to go even though neither of us had finished lunch. It was one of the few things that would upset him. He was proud of his profession, and though he never mentioned it to the offending stranger, he and I knew his drawing of funny pictures was giving him a yearly income high in six figures.

Most cartoonists work at home and are underfoot daily. Their wives have to be patient and also recognize the work pressures on their husbands. It takes understanding to recognize that an afternoon nap is not laziness, but usually begins with a concentrated period of working on ideas. I am lucky in this—Nadia, the girl from high school, is an artist with a love of cartoonists and their work. This makes the erratic life style succeed. We inherited the night work habit from Segar, and we still dash out at three in the morning for a hamburger.

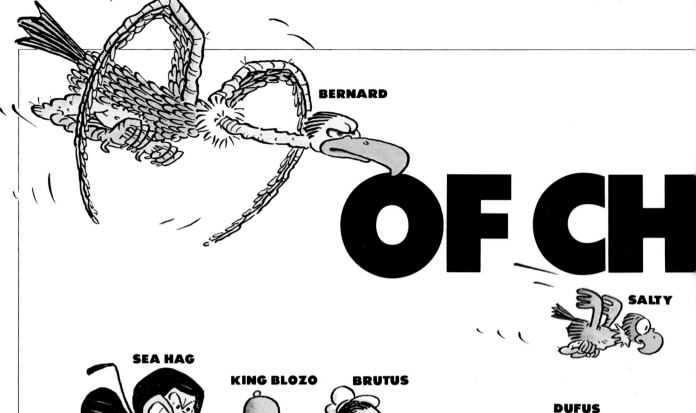

BERNARD

OF CH

SALTY

SEA HAG

KING BLOZO

BRUTUS

COLE OYL

DUFUS

GHOST

PROFESSOR O. G.
WATASNOZZLE

CASTOR OYL

EUGENE THE JEEP

NANA OYL

JOHN SAPI

THE CAST ARACTERS

BERNICE THE WHIFFLE HEN

ALICE THE GOON

OLIVE OYL

J. WELLINGTON WIMPY

POPEYE

POOPDECK PAPPY

PLANT FEED

SPINACH

VITAMINS

SWEE'PEA

GRANNY

SPINACH

POPEYE

Popeye is a perfect example of a creative person's brainchild taking over and controlling the actions of its creator. As with so many other Segar characters, Popeye was never intended to be anything but a temporary addition to the cast. Castor Oyl and Ham Gravy needed a sailor for their ship, and a comic character was essential to the story—to be used for a few laughs and then dropped.

In his first few months of existence, the new character showed little evidence of the strong, fist-swinging fighter he was to become. On the contrary, during this period, Popeye indicated a tendency to act on the cautious, if not cowardly side. He was nothing but a hired hand, working for the stars of the feature.

Segar often said it was Popeye's first attempt to fend off a monster that began his metamorphosis. The humor and action of the fat arms swinging and landing thunderous blows brought to his creator's awareness the fact that he had inadvertently added a natural fighter to the strip.

Even with this knowledge, there was still no intention of permitting Popeye to stay in the feature—the strip was doing fine with the stars it had. Segar had just signed a contract with a substantial increase in salary, so why complicate a good thing? A new major character might upset the already well-established theme so solidly set by Castor Oyl, Ham Gravy

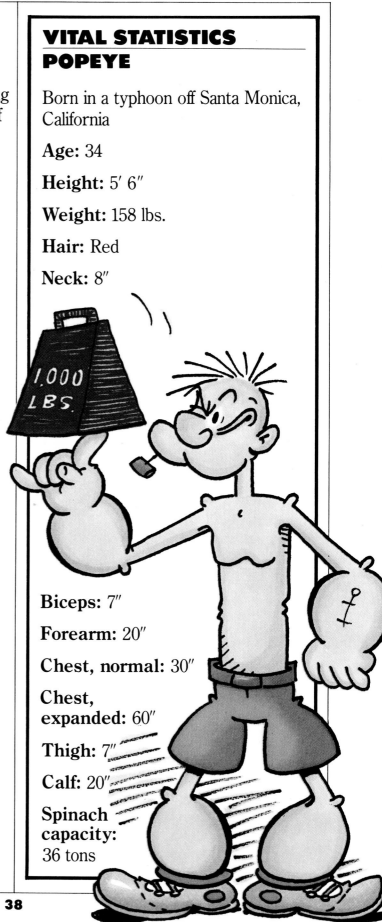

VITAL STATISTICS
POPEYE

Born in a typhoon off Santa Monica, California

Age: 34

Height: 5′ 6″

Weight: 158 lbs.

Hair: Red

Neck: 8″

Biceps: 7″

Forearm: 20″

Chest, normal: 30″

Chest, expanded: 60″

Thigh: 7″

Calf: 20″

Spinach capacity: 36 tons

and Olive Oyl.

But Segar had underestimated his own instinct. He had accidentally produced an element that wouldn't stay dropped, and a new story had barely begun to develop when he found himself reinserting the sailor into the strip. This time Popeye was there to stay, and THIMBLE THEATRE had a new star in its cast.

Associating so closely with Popeye and his creator, learning to know and understand them both, I gradually became aware that philosophically the character and the man were one. Popeye's fundamental honesty and loyalty—his absolute belief in right and wrong, with no grays—were but reflections of Segar. All creative people put a part of themselves into their work; it would be difficult not to. With Popeye, Segar continually expressed his own feelings about villains, crooked politicians, dictators and skulduggery in any form opposed to his standards.

Few characters in real life or literature have loved with such fierce devotion as Popeye. For fifty years, his overwhelming protective feeling for his pickle-nosed sweety, backed by his famous "twisker sock," has provided readers around the world with a model of true affection. At times, Popeye may seem neglectful of Olive, and with his tunnel vision these are normal, human interruptions with no bearing on his love. Boats do need to be painted; new monsters must be destroyed and the downtrodden championed. But Olive is never out of Popeye's thoughts.

The sailor isn't always as secure in Olive's love as he'd like to be. He is capable of jealousy, and the results are physical—a typhoon is a gentle summer breeze compared to the total destruction he wreaks on anyone foolish enough to woo his sweety.

The decision to make Popeye a professional fighter was a natural step in his development as a character. Segar was a fight fan, and the late twenties and thirties were a period of important heavyweight contests. When Segar discovered he had a great natural fighter, the logical step was to have him turn professional.

Popeye moved into true star status gradually, and his creator was unaware of the sailor's impact on the comic-reading public. It wasn't until 1932 that Segar began to fully realize what had happened with his strip. By then, the fan mail had increased, radio comedians were including Popeye jokes in their routines, and royalty checks were arriving for toys, games and novelties.

There was no longer any doubt—Popeye was popular with the public at large. The sailor with the spinach-arms had shoved Ham Gravy and Castor Oyl aside and was now the undisputed star of THIMBLE THEATRE.

LOVE COMES TO A SAILOR

On August 27, 1929, several months after Popeye's first appearance in THIMBLE THEATRE, an event took place that was destined not only to change the direction of the feature, but also to change forever the life of the one-eyed sailor. The momentous event was a kiss on the side of Popeye's fat chin from Castor Oyl's sister, Olive.

This romantic incident was a mistake on the part of Olive. The lovesick girl imagined she was kissing Julius J. Herringbone, her current romantic interest. To Olive it was only a careless blunder—but to Popeye it

Olive approaches

The kiss

A mistake?

Love!   SEGAR: AUGUST 27, 1929

was love at first kiss. Until this time, he had thought of Olive as an unnecessary sister of his friend Castor Oyl. The unexpected, glorious kiss transformed his indifference. For the first time in his life, true love had come to Popeye the sailor man.

This simple kiss signaled the death knell for one of THIMBLE THEATRE's original cast. Poor Ham Gravy, who had loyally loved his skinny girl friend for ten years, would be cast aside by Olive, to be replaced by the sailor he and Castor had hired as a one-man crew.

Ham Gravy hasn't been forgotten completely. Several times in recent years, he has been brought back to create situations where the intensity of Popeye's jealousy can be shown.

Spinach capital Crystal City, Texas, erected this statue in the 1930's to honor E. C. Segar and Popeye for their influence on America's eating habits

YUM!

SPINACH

Segar needed a logical explanation for Popeye's fighting prowess and superhuman strength. He chose spinach—a natural selection, since doctors in the late twenties were extolling the benefits of the green weed. It was full of iron and other healthy things, they said, and should be eaten by everyone for strength and vitality.

Because of their love and admiration for Popeye, children who had detested spinach were now demanding it. How could parents disagree with doctors *and* Popeye?

From 1931 to 1936, the spinach industry credited Segar and Popeye with increasing the United States consumption of spinach by 33 percent.

In well-meaning but overenthusiastic appreciation, every few days the spinach growers shipped a crate of fresh spinach to the Segar home. No one family could consume the quantity of spinach the Segars received, and it was given to friends and neighbors—who began avoiding the family and their kind gifts. Finally, a diplomatic letter put a stop to the spinach flow, and everyone returned to a normal diet.

July 6, '78

Dear Sir:
Our little son Jimmy loves Popeye and because of it we have a serious problem.
HE WONT EAT ANYTHING BUT SPINACH!!
Will you please have Popeye write to him and tell him there are other healthy things he should eat?
Sincerely
Mrs. Marjorie Hill

A sample of many letters received from troubled parents

POPEYE WRITES ABOUT HIMSELF

By E. C. SEGAR, 1936

TO ME FRIEN'S....
THEY'S A LOT OF THINGS WHICH FOLKS DON'T KNOW ABOUT ME .... EVER'BODY KNOWS I YAM STRONG, BUT NOBODY KNOWS HOW STRONG EXCEP' MESELF.... BY USING ME SPECIAL TWISKER SOCK I KIN KNOCK AN ELEPHINK CLEAN ORF'N HIS FEET ....SLAPPIN' DOWN A HORSH AIN'T ABSOLUKELY NOTHIN' .... I NEVER HITS A MAN AS HARD AS I KIN ON ACCOUNT OF IT AIN'T RIGHT TO KILL PEOPLES .... I USUALLY WEIGHS ABOUT A HUN'RED AN' FIFTY-EIGHT POUNDS... I YAM FIVE FEET SIX TALL .... THE REASING I WEIGHS MORE'N YA THINK IS ON ACCOUNT OF ME MUSKLES IS JUS' LIKE STEEL CABLES ..... I BEEN SHOT A HUN'ERD AN' TWENTY TIMES ....AN' I AIN'T DEAD YET .... WHEN A BULLIT DOES GO THROUGH ME TOUGH HIDE IT DON'T BOTHER ME NONE ....CEPTIN' I HAS TO CORK UP THE HOLE ON ACCOUNT OF I DON'T LIKE DRAFTS BLOWIN' THROUGH ME .... RIGHT NOW THEY'S TWENTY-SEVEN BULLIT IN ME WICH IS ANOTHER REASON I WEIGHS MORE'N

WHAT IT LOOKS LIKE AS IF I DO.... I BEEN STABBED NINE HUN'ERD AN' TWEN'Y-TWO TIMES AN' THA'S HOW MANY KNIVES WITCH GOT RUIN'D......I DRUNK CARBOLICAL ACID ONCET AN' IT DIDN'T HURT ME ON ACCOUNT OF I GOT A STUMICK LIKE NOBODY'S BUSINESS....I GOT MILLINGS AN' MILLINGS OF FRIEN'S AN' I ONLY GOT TWENTY-SIX THOUSING EMENIES... ONE NIGHT I KILLED TWEN'Y-ONE PIRITS....I AIN'T GOT NO SYMPTHITY FER PIRITS THA'S WHY I POPS 'EM ORF WIT' ME SPECIAL TWISKERS SOCK...... SOMEDAY I'LL TELL YA HOW I LOS' ME RIGHT EYE ...IT WAS THE MOS' ARFUL BATTLE OF ME WHOLE LIFE... I HAD MORE FUN THAT NIGHT.... ARF! ARF! THA'S ALL I YAM GONER TELL YA ON ACCOUNT OF YA'D HAVE NIGHT MARES ALL DAY LONG IF I TOLD YA ABOUT SOME OF ME HORREEBLE EXPERIENCES!

POPEYE

POPEYE'S FAMOUS PUNCHES OF HISTORY

Note: No punches thrown at Brutus are shown—everyday events have no place in history

THE TWISKER SOCK

Warning: Do not attempt without aid of spinach

1. Arm is brought back and wound in counterclockwise direction

2. As offensive weapon starts forward, unwinding action begins

3. Arm and fist, like spinning bullet, are held on direct line target

4. With power in all directions, Twisker Sock lands and objective is destroyed

OXHEART, 1933

JABBO, March 25, 1930

EMOK, 1971

POPEYE'S FIRST PUNCH, February 18, 1929

OCTOPUS, October 22, 1936

GENERAL BUNZO, 1931

SEA HAG'S VULTURE, January 5, 1937

BOLO, March 16, 1937

BRUTALITY

As the theme of strength and spinach-muscles grew, Popeye tended more and more to strike out at anything he feared or didn't understand. Animals, people and even inanimate objects were targets for his fast-acting fists. The philosophy "Hit 'em first and they can't hurt ya!" was the basis for much of his humor in early years and was responsible for a large percentage of his gain in popularity.

Though today it may seem brutal, Popeye's outlook was a natural reaction of the times. A population frustrated by the Great Depression liked the idea of one small man fighting back and winning. They, too, wanted to strike out at something they feared and didn't understand.

Even poor dumb animals weren't safe from the swinging fists of the early sailor man

SEGAR: DECEMBER 23, 1930

IN THE EARLY 1930'S, AN UNFORESEEN EVENT TOOK PLACE—

the children of America fell in love with a sailor

ORDERS FROM W. R. HEARST

It was my habit as Segar's assistant to arrive at his home about noon, in time for a quiet breakfast and a leisurely discussion of the day's work. Never having seen him angry or violently upset, I was startled one day in 1934 to encounter a black atmosphere and my employer in an even darker mood. He had just received a telegram from the president of King Features. Segar stopped his pacing long enough to shake the yellow paper under my nose. "Read it!" he ordered.

The wire is long-lost, but in essence it read: "Hearst says Popeye is loved by the children of America … Stop his swearing … Stop his brutality … Make him respectable." These commands could not have been more unexpected or harder to take than if the syndicate had given orders to make Olive a sex symbol. "The fun will be gone," Segar muttered. "There's nothing funny about a sissy sailor!"

A decree from "the Chief" was not to be ignored—so Popeye's language was softened and his random smacking without a cause was modified. He was almost made a gentleman.

THE NEW POPEYE

The new Popeye is plainly shown in this portion from a 1936 continuity introducing Eugene the Jeep. Rarely now does the hard-hitting sailor strike out without a just cause.

The villainous Mister Chizzleflint has hired "Slag the Slugger" to steal the Jeep from Olive. When Slag encounters Popeye in Olive's home, a terrible battle ensues. In the midst of the furious action, Segar took time out to assure the reader that Popeye is fighting on the right side.

Hitting without a cause wasn't the image of a hero

SEGAR: MAY 13, 1936

AND THE WINNAH IS . . .

SEGAR: SEPTEMBER 1, 1935

SPINACH-MUSCLES

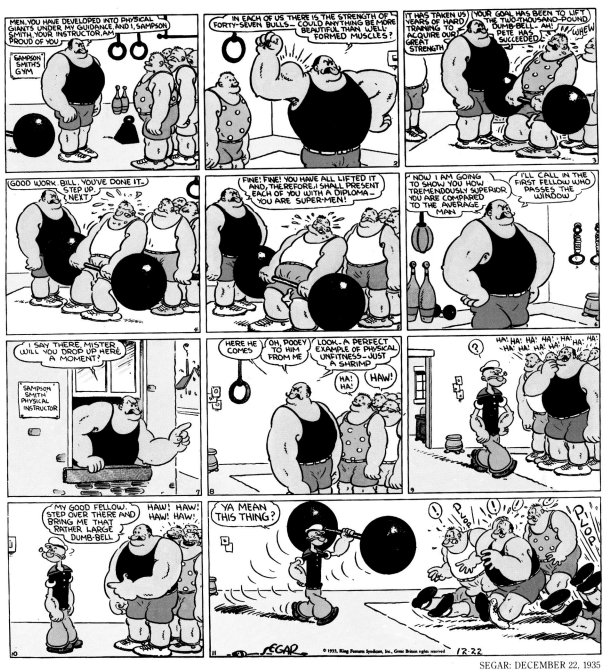

SEGAR: DECEMBER 22, 1935

SAGENDORF: NOVEMBER 26, 1978

EDJAMACATION IS FUN

SAGENDORF: JUNE 5, 1960

VITAL STATISTICS
MISS OLIVE OYL

Born in New York City

Age: 29

Height: 5′10⅞″

Weight: 96 lbs., 3 oz.

Neck: Swan

Nose: Pickle

Arms: Long

Ankles: Two

Shoe size: 14AAAAAA

Chemical composition:
101% woman

19-19-19

OLIVE OYL

Helen of Troy's beauty may have launched a thousand ships, but the willowy, pickle-nosed star of THIMBLE THEATRE has helped launch over twenty times that many daily cartoons in her sixty years of existence. Olive is all women. True, she may not have the looks of a Marilyn Monroe, Mae West or Dolly Parton. But inside, where it really counts, she is all of these and much more.

To Olive, life is simple—except when she complicates it. After ten years with Ham Gravy as her boyfriend, she found in Popeye a man who can solve any senseless problem she creates for herself. Not that Olive is stupid. She is an independent thinker with an overactive imagination, and she invites situations that call for the strength of a spinach-eating sailor.

Olive's love for her Popeye is as unyielding and perpetual as any woman's for her sailor. Of course, there are moments when jewels, great wealth or flattery threaten to divert her feelings, but these lapses are short-lived. Popeye is her man. The few times other women have shown interest in him, Olive has protected her property as fiercely as her sailor boy ever fought with his fists.

As Popeye's importance grew, so did his relationship with Olive. Their love affair started slowly; both took a long time to notice and become interested in the other. Once on their way, however, there was no stopping them. They were a team.

Olive has held firmly to her role of leading lady, and today her position is more secure than ever. Solid in her stardom and protected by the love of her sailor, she has everything—no woman could ask for more.

Every day in these changing times, we are confronted with something new or faced with the loss of something old. It is comforting to know that even though hemlines of women's skirts go up and down, Olive's always remain the same.

Proof-positive that beauty is only skin-deep

OLIVE MEETS GLINT GORE

In this segment from a 1930–31 continuity, Segar portrays the complete personality of Olive Oyl—from helpless female to ferocious fighter. The segment also illustrates Segar's ability to deviate from the main theme—in this instance, a detective story—to side episodes without destroying the plot.

The meeting

Popeye leaves the scene

SEGAR: JANUARY 12, 1931

Helpless fear and a cry for help

A helpless female …

SEGAR: JANUARY 13, 1931

… must defend herself

She gets indignant

SEGAR: JANUARY 14, 1931

*She knows she's a helpless female and
he's no gentleman*

*But he's caught her
interest ... she's curious*

A horrible revelation

SEGAR: JANUARY 19, 1931

It's time to get serious

Concern … tenderness … the mother instinct

SEGAR: JANUARY 21, 1931

Relief

Back to indignation

Don't worry, Popeye arrives in time to save his helpless sweety

THE ROMANTIC

SEGAR: DECEMBER 26, 1937

WHA'S GOOD FOR THE GOOSE . . .

SEGAR: APRIL 12, 1936

FALSE ALARM

SAGENDORF: JULY 11, 1965

66

CLOTHESHORSH

SAGENDORF: MAY 2, 1965

67

Li'l Swee'pea was left on Popeye's doorstep by his mother

Of royal birth, he needed protection from an evil uncle

He still wears a nightgown, and he still can't kick a feetball

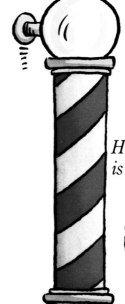

His greatest ambition is to need a haircut

SWEE'PEA

Swee'pea's popularity has grown steadily since his first appearance in 1933. Today, he is particularly popular with college students. Perhaps it is his mild opposition to his "adopted" father's authority. He does get tired of his daily diet of spinach—he knows ice cream has just as many "vitamings" and tastes better. And he likes Olive Oyl, but she does interfere in his time with Popeye.

When the subject of Popeye's li'l Swee'pea comes up in conversation, a debate is bound to follow. Where did Popeye get him? Who is he/she? Swee'pea is definitely not the offspring of Olive and Popeye. He does live with Popeye, and the sailor feeds him spinach and teaches him many of his fisticuff tactics. As to gender, he is unquestionably a boy-child—and anyone in doubt will get one of his baby spinach-punches. For the rest, the explanation is involved.

Segar contributed to the confusion by giving the baby two backgrounds. In his first appearance, Swee'pea has been sent by express to Popeye for safekeeping from the Demonian Secret Service. Demonians are a superstitious people, and they want the baby because he has seven moles on his back—five on one side and two on the other, the total resembling a pair of dice with a lucky seven. (In later continuities, the moles must have vanished; his back is used for purposes such as pirate maps and secret messages.) Certain that Swee'pea is a symbol of good fortune, the Demonians intend to make him an object of worship.

In the later version of Swee'pea's first appearance, his father has been killed and he has been made Crown Prince of Demonia. A mean old uncle wants to eliminate the royal baby and thus gain complete control of the country. Swee'pea's mother sneaks him across the border and leaves him on Popeye's doorstep, knowing the trustworthy sailor will protect him.

An often-asked question is, Why doesn't Swee'pea grow up? The characters in THIMBLE THEATRE are symbols whose actions stay true to their individual and definite personalities. A character's looks may change slightly as time goes by, but the behavior will never fail to reflect the comic character's own personal identity. Wimpy will always mooch hamburgers, Geezil will always hate Wimpy "to pieces," and Brutus will never stop trying to defeat Popeye.

Segar held these beliefs, and so do I. Swee'pea will not grow up but will remain a loving and loyal "adopted" baby for Popeye to guide and protect.

Yes! He does have feet!

TWO OF 'EM!

SWEE'PEA'S FIRST APPEARANCE

The mysterious box from Swee'pea's mother was opened by Popeye on July 28, 1933. It's contents may have been a surprise to the sailor, but from his reaction not an unwelcome one.

SEGAR: JULY 28, 1933

SEGAR: AUGUST 17, 1933

THE CHRISTENING

It was Segar's intention to name the baby Schooner, but Popeye won out with his continued use of the endearment "Me li'l Swee'pea".

WELL, BLOW ME DOWN!!

Swee'pea's first spoken words, June 23, 1938

THE MATERNAL INSTINCT

SEGAR: JULY 19, 1936

THE REAL MOTHER SHOWS UP

The arrival of Swee'pea's mother to claim her baby caused Segar a great deal of trouble. Having fallen into the nasty trap of creating for the sake of a few funny gags, he found himself faced with the moral problem of an unrelated sailor and a mother fighting over who would have permanent possession of the child. The situation produced some extremely funny moments, and yet there were touching scenes with Swee'pea screaming to stay with Popeye, a wailing mother, and the sailor torn between love for the baby and his stricken conscience.

Eventually, Segar felt the humor had been bled out of the story line, and he was ready to move on to something new. The problem had to be resolved. Swee'pea was much too valuable as a character to be returned to his mother and dropped from the strip—but to leave them both in might create another strong female character, and Olive would never permit that.

The troublesome situation was solved by quietly dropping the mother and not mentioning her again. If readers protested the cruel and inhuman act of separating a baby from his mother, she could always be restored to the strip. The expected protests never materialized. Li'l Swee'pea had become so popular and firmly established in Popeye's life that the readers were apparently willing to have him become motherless.

J. WELLINGTON WIMPY

With his twenty-four college degrees and lofty IQ, Wimpy is the most misunderstood member of the THIMBLE THEATRE family. The character who gave us the famous "I'll gladly pay you Tuesday for a hamburger today" is regarded by many readers and students of comic art as nothing more than a fat, lazy, stupid fool. But one has only to look at his immense girth to recognize the degree of success he has achieved in his chosen profession of mooching. It takes the skill of a master con artist, and an understanding of human vulnerability far beyond that of the average psychologist, to accumulate such mass without working a single day.

J. Wellington Wimpy appeared physically, though nameless, in THE FIVE-FIFTEEN comic strip, but not until Popeye came along did he become a regular in THIMBLE THEATRE. When Popeye began to fight professionally in

What Popeye did for spinach, Wimpy did for the lowly hamburger

Bill Schuchert was clearly one of the models for J. Wellington Wimpy

the early thirties, it became necessary to create a referee. Segar brought the fat man's image forward from THE FIVE-FIFTEEN, gave him a personality and a name, and introduced him as the referee in Popeye's fights.

Many citizens of Segar's birthplace believe that Wimpy's outward appearance was modeled after Bill Schuchert, Segar's kind boss at the Chester Opera House. Mrs. Jessie Lee Huffstutler, who played the piano at the opera house, recalls Schuchert's love of hamburgers and that he would send young Segar to get them.

Wimpy's reflection of Segar's boss ends with his physical likeness and his love of hamburgers. His basic character was taken from a prizefight referee seen weekly at the Ocean Park, California, sports arena. This obnoxious man would enter the ring to the sound of boos and catcalls. Ducking flying objects (he once dodged a ladies' shoe thrown by an

I'LL HAVE PICKLE, LETTUCE AND ONION BOTH PLEASE, ON THE NEXT DOZEN!

VITAL STATISTICS
J. WELLINGTON WIMPY

Born in a hamburger joint, Ocean Park Pier, California

Age: 34

Weight: 300 hamburgers

Hat size: Jumbo hamburger

Waist: 18 hamburgers

Height: 26 hamburgers

IQ: 326

Tummy capacity: Unlimited

angry Mrs. Segar), he would introduce himself in a voice much louder and clearer than his mild, delayed in troduction of the contestants. There were rumors that his income was greatly increased by his prefight knowledge of contest results. These characteristics are, and have always been, part of J. Wellington Wimpy's behavior when refereeing Popeye's battles in the ring.

From a creative point of view,

Wimpy has always been a problem. Segar often tried to write Sunday gags in which the sailor would get the best of the moocher. Many nights, we'd think we had laid out a page where this would happen, but the next day, starting to work on the penciled Sunday page, I would find that Wimpy had again foxed Popeye. When questioned, Segar's answer was always the same: "It just happened. Wimpy is smarter than Popeye—he has to win."

Popeye's attitude toward his fat pal is simple. Wimpy's mooching may drive the sailor "nerts," but in his own words, "Frien's is the mos' importink thing on eart', even if ya can't stan' 'em!"

THE REFEREE

NOW, GENTLEMEN, LET'S YOU AND HIM FIGHT

BONG

THE FIGHT IS ON! — THEY CIRCLE AND EYE EACH OTHER LIKE TWO BEASTS —

POPEYE FEINTS WITH HIS LEFT — KID MUSTARD PULLS IN HIS CHIN AND COVERS UP LIKE A TURTLE — THE BOYS HAVE A LOT OF RESPECT FOR EACH OTHER — BOTH ARE SPINACH EATERS —

RATHER AN UNINTERESTING FIGHT — THEY WEAVE, BOB, DUCK AND DANCE — BUT NOT A BLOW STRUCK — HO-HUM —

J. WELLINGTON WIMPY, THE REFEREE, SLEEPS SOUNDLY IN A NEUTRAL CORNER

POPEYE LOWERS HIS GUARD, STICKS OUT HIS CHIN AND INVITES A SOCK

THE KID SWINGS A TERRIFIC RIGHT BUT MISSES BY INCHES AS POPEYE PULLS IN HIS NECK —

THEN POPEYE'S GLOVE EXPLODES IN THE KID'S FACE LIKE A BOMB —

WHO SHOT?

NOBODY SHOT — I JUS' HIT HIM SO HARD ME GLOVE EXPLODED LIKE A PAPER BAG FULL OF AIR

I'LL OBTAIN ANOTHER GLOVE FOR YOU

AND NOW, MY GOOD PEOPLE I WILL GIVE AN —

?

2-21

— IMITATION OF A MALE ROBIN — "TWEET - TWEET" FEMALE — "TWEET TWEET"

ORIOLE — TWEET TWEET"

IMITATION OF A HORSE — "TWEET - TWEET"

A FISH — "TWEET - TWEET"

SEGAR FEBRUARY 21, 1937

PERPETUAL PEST

SEGAR: MAY 24, 1936

77

FOLLOWING ORDERS

SAGENDORF: MAY 27, 1973

WIMPY ALWAYS WINS

I'LL HAVE A HAMBURGER IF WIMPY AIN'T AROUN'!

YOU'D BETTER EAT IT FAST...IT'S ABOUT TIME FOR HIM TO SHOW!

I HAVEN'T HAD A HAMBURGER IN TWO DAYS!

YA AIN'T MOOCHIN' ME!

NO! NO! YOU MISUNDERSTAND! I HAVE GIVEN UP THE GROUND COW!

I AM TRAINING MYSELF TO RESIST THE SALUBRIOUS BUN AND MEAT!

BLOW ME DOWN!?! 'AT'S GREAT, WIMPY!!

IT **IS** A CHALLENGE, SIR!!

LE'S TEST YER INTERMAL FORTITUBES!!

A PLEASURE, OL' FRIEND!

BEANS

HOW AM I DOING, OL' PAL?

JUS' GREAT! I YAM PROUD OF YA!!

BEANS

© King Features Syndicate, Inc., 1977. World rights reserved.

NICE-SMELLING LITTLE RASCAL, ISN'T IT?

SNIFF!

GULP!!

I GUESS STRENGTH OF CHARACTER IS NOT ONE OF MY VIRTUES!

9-11

SAGENDORF: SEPTEMBER 11, 1977

VITAL STATISTICS
BRUTUS

Born in Hollywood, California

Age: 36

Height: 6'8"

Weight: 372 lbs.

Head: Empty

Neck: 22"

Jaw: Glass

Reach: Irrelevant

Waist: 62"

Posture: Horizontal, especially when Popeye makes contact with his nose or jaw

BRUTUS

The monstrous Brutus, with his overwhelming desire to defeat Popeye, was created by Segar for animated films in the mid-thirties. The animation studio needed a continuing villain to form a triangle with Olive and the sailor—someone who would be there to compete for love of the fair Olive. When the studio requested a new character, it fell to me to research all the tough men Popeye had fought in the newspaper strips. Then, with a pile of defeated characters in front of him, Segar created a composite villain—one big enough to afford Popeye a continuing rival.

In films and television, Brutus is called Bluto. In the fifties, after a disagreement over the origin of the name, he became known as Brutus— in comic books and newspaper strips. Because of his tremendous popularity, the bearded giant was made a member of the cast in the newspaper feature and continues his record of losing fights on a regular basis.

Brutus is not dumb—he's just plain stupid. After years of being flattened by Popeye's fists, he still thinks he can be victorious over the sailor. Even Olive and li'l Swee'pea have floored him with single punches, but he refuses to recognize that he was born with a glass jaw.

From a cartoonist's point of view, Brutus is a great character to work with. His large body and small brain lend themselves to humorous situations and action that is fun to draw— particularly if you enjoy drawing characters flat on their backs.

A HARD MAN TO KNOCK DOWN

SAGENDORF: MARCH 19, 1972

Sometimes Brutus wins

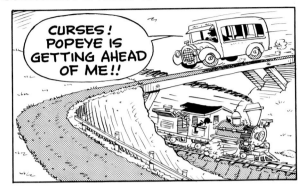

But not without Popeye's help

85

EUGENE THE JEEP

The small yellow animal Olive received from her Uncle Ben on March 3, 1936, has proven through the years to be universally the most popular of THIMBLE THEATRE's menagerie. Eugene the Jeep was a departure from Segar's usual creatures. Most of the side beasts were anything but pleasant in physical appearance. Added as heavies, their purpose was to challenge Popeye and put fear in the hearts of readers. With the Jeep, Segar took the opposite direction. He wanted—and created— an animal that was charming in looks and pleasant in personality. Only villains have anything to fear from Eugene.

The creation of this appealing animal was the most exciting and pleasing experience of my years with Segar. The Jeep was magic. From the first rough sketches through to the naming, the small creature insisted on being born.

After settling on the physical design of the new character, we had to decide what to call him. At breakfast one morning, as we were mulling over possible names, one entry on Segar's list stood out like a neon sign: "Jeep." There was no doubt; that was it, instantly as natural as calling a dog a dog. We checked English and foreign dictionaries to be sure it wasn't in use, then chose the name once and for all—and added a new word to the language.

Later, when asked about a first name, I suggested Eugene. I had personal reasons for its use and was delighted when it was accepted.

No attempt will be made here to explain what Jeeps are or where they come from. Professor Brainstine, in Eugene's first appearance in the Sunday comics on August 9, 1936 (reprinted on page 89), gives a full and comprehensive answer to these questions.

Eugene the Jeep doesn't live with Popeye; he's usually busy ruling Jeep Island. But because of his ability to foretell the future, the little animal always appears when Popeye or Swee'pea needs his special talents.

How the Jeep answers questions

SEGAR: AUGUST 3, 1936

It took days of
wondering before the
family got up enough
nerve to find out what
was in the mysterious
package Olive
received from the
famous explorer,
Uncle Ben Oyl.

SEGAR: MARCH 21, 1936

SEGAR: APRIL 1, 1936

There was no
connection between
the Jeep's first
appearance and
April Fools' Day.

Eugene was an
instant success with
both the comic-strip
family and the
reading public.

SEGAR: APRIL 2, 1936

WHA'S A JEEP?

SEGAR: AUGUST 9, 1936

Eugene's Sunday feature debut was the occasion for a precise description of the true African Jeep.

The one thing he ain't is a "blastid" gentleman

There is no love lost between Pappy and his son's sweety

POOPDECK PAPPY

The creation of Poopdeck Pappy in 1936 was a direct result of orders to soften Popeye and turn him into a gentleman hero. The character change deprived Segar of the fun he had with Popeye's slam-bam, rough and often crude humor, and he was determined to do something to make up for the loss. He decided to create a character who would make Popeye at his worst look like a sissy. And create one he did. Poopdeck Pappy's lack of respect for women, law, relations and honesty was completely foreign to the nasty old man's son.

In an early Pappy story, the unscrupulous old tar opens Popeye's safe, steals his son's life savings and with his ill-gotten wealth purchases a huge diamond ring for his new girl friend. Standing at the end of a dock in glowing moonlight, he slips the ring on the lady's finger, then takes her in his arms and kisses her willing lips. Suddenly he pulls back, picks up the girl and tosses her into the ocean:

she's been eating onions. The result of this action is a prolonged court trial; and Pappy is sent to jail—an experience he thoroughly enjoys.

And Pappy has continued his unprincipled behavior. In a recent episode, Popeye catches his father in the dishonest business of making anchors of wood, painting them metal-gray and selling the worthless objects to unsuspecting shipowners.

Naturally, Pappy blames his illegal operations on his stingy son. A chronic complaint of "the old goat" is that his allowance isn't enough to cover tobacco costs—nor enough for him to enjoy the nightlife he feels entitled to.

The addition of Popeye's Granny to the household has had a slight controlling influence on Pappy. To Granny he is still her little boy, and she tries her best to raise her eighty-nine-year-old son to be a proper gentleman.

The feud between Pappy and Olive is constant. Pappy can't understand a son of his loving a "lath-legged bean pole," and Olive has never forgiven him for smacking her around the first time they met.

Eugene the Jeep helps Popeye find his long-lost father

SEGAR: OCTOBER 24, 1936

Pappy's reaction to being found isn't exactly what Popeye expected or hoped for

SEGAR: OCTOBER 27, 1936

SEGAR: OCTOBER 29, 1936

Pappy believes in keeping females in their place

SEGAR: NOVEMBER 11, 1936

But he's still attracted to what he considers the weaker sex

SEGAR: NOVEMBER 21, 1936

PAPPY EXPLAINS

With typical Poopdeck logic, the long-missing Pappy tells why he ran off and left his baby son without a father.

POPPA, I WANTS TO AST YA SUMPIN'— HOW COME YOU AN' ME HAS BEEN SEPERATED SO LONG?

WELL, FORTY YEARS AGO WHEN YE WAS ABOUT TWO YEARS OLD I SENT YE OUT TO BUY ME A COB PIPE—

BUT YE DIDN'T COME BACK

I WAITED AN' WAITED, BUT YE DIDN'T COME BACK

© 1936 King Features Syndicate, Inc.
World rights reserved

SO I PACKS UP, GETS ABOARD ME SHIP AN' SAILS AWAY

YE BRAT!

FORTY YEARS AGO

DID YA WAIT A LONG TIME FOR ME TO COME BACK BEFORE YA SAILED AWAY AN' LEFT ME?

I SURE DID—

I WAITED TILL SIX O'CLOCK

SEGAR: NOVEMBER 6, 1936

94

SEGAR: NOVEMBER 4, 1936

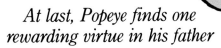

*At last, Popeye finds one
rewarding virtue in his father*

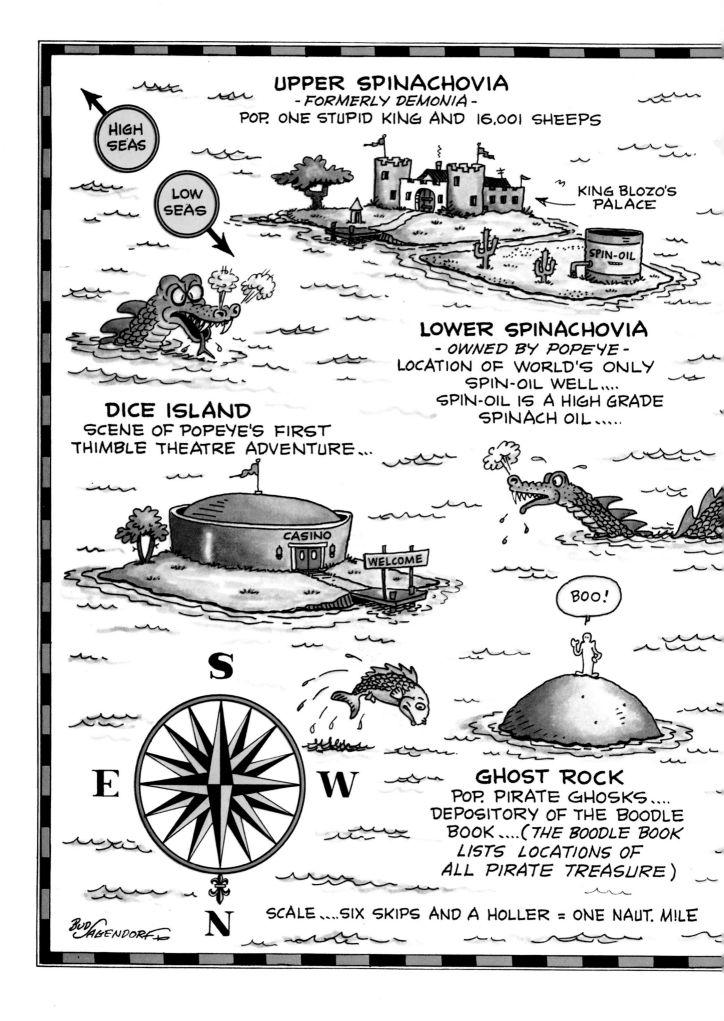

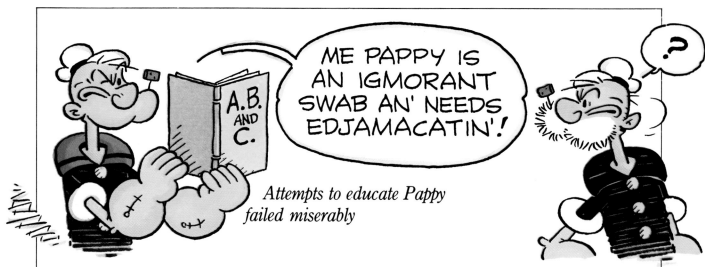

Attempts to educate Pappy
failed miserably

SAGENDORF: SEPTEMBER 4, 1959

SAGENDORF: AUGUST 24, 1959

SAGENDORF: SEPTEMBER 17, 1959

98

UNPRINCIPLED

SAGENDORF: JANUARY 26, 1964

FAMILY PRIDE

SAGENDORF: OCTOBER 8, 1961

She talks in oscilloscope language

Kicked out of the strip as horrible monster

She returns in clothes and becomes Swee'pea's baby-sitter

ALICE THE GOON

On a Sunday morning in 1934, a weird apparition was delivered to millions of American homes as part of the comic section in the Sunday newspaper: Alice the Goon had arrived. Not only did she bring evil and fear into the hearts of her readers; she also brought a new word to dictionaries. "Goon" has become part of our language and is credited to the hairy monster's, creator, Segar.

Alice appeared first as a slave of the Sea Hag, Popeye's eternal enemy. The idea was that the horrible beast would eventually meet Popeye, a classic battle would take place and the creature would be disposed of. This was not to be the case. Alice eventually made a home for herself and remains an important member of the cast.

Probably no cartoon character in the past had ever created the overwhelming response that Alice the Goon produced. Segar had done it again, but this time it wasn't a humorous Wimpy, a grumpy Pappy or a cute little Swee'pea baby boy. It was a monster of evil. The bloated, nude body, the hairy legs and arms, were repulsive and terrifying. The words in the balloons over her head were inhuman. They resembled images on an oscilloscope—wiggly, vertical lines—and proved she was definitely not of earthly origin.

After only a few appearances, newspapers across the country started getting letters of protest. The hairy monster was frightening small children, and parents were warning their offspring, "Be good or the Goon will get you!" Comic strips are not intended to scare readers, and a stop order was received from the syndicate to drop poor Alice. As with the order to soften Popeye, this was a blow to Segar. The problem of Alice's future was settled quite simply. After a respectable length of time, Alice was brought back, more human now, clothed in a blouse and skirt, wearing a hat with a perky flower. On her return and in her new image, she became attached to li'l Swee'pea, beat up the evil Sea Hag and settled down to become the family baby-sitter.

Wimpy is the only human who understands Goon talk

A HORRIBLE MONSTER

THE NEW ALICE

THE SEA HAG

The malevolent Sea Hag, the last true witch on earth, has been Popeye's number one enemy since she first appeared on December 26, 1929. She is determined to bring piracy back to the high seas, but her plots and evil designs to eliminate Popeye continue to be her main, wicked purpose in life.

The importance of a *real* witch to the story line of THIMBLE THEATRE cannot be overemphasized. The Sea Hag's genuine black powers permit the logical use of magic in her perpetual battle against good and Popeye. Without this magic, many of the humorous situations and plots would become silly and fanciful, and totally out of place in a comic strip using satire as its basic theme.

In the conflict between the Sea Hag and Popeye, all the advantages are on the side of the witch—she has her magic, an evil mind and her pet vulture, Bernard. Popeye has only spinach and his firm belief in right and wrong as foils against her attempts to defeat him. His gallant respect for all women is another stumbling block in his efforts to finish off this insidious "emeny." Witches are women, and no matter how vile the Sea Hag is, Popeye can't smack or even slap her. When fisticuffs are called for, it's usually Olive who takes over and does physical damage to the witch.

SEGAR: DECEMBER 26, 1929

The Sea Hag's first appearance

The Sea Hag's true feelings about Popeye are hard to understand. On one hand, her aim in life is to destroy him. But when it looks like she might have succeeded, she crumbles into a fit of depression as if she's lost a loved one.

The old Hag suffers from one personal problem. As the last witch on earth, she has no friends. When her rare yearnings for company occur, she joyfully pays an unwelcome visit to Popeye's home. Popeye finds these unexpected visits upsetting, and Granny is even more disturbed. Popeye's grandmother may be the world's worst cook, but she doesn't use lizards and gnat's eyes in her culinary endeavors—the Sea Hag does.

A true witch has trouble in the modern world

FLYING LESSONS

SAGENDORF: OCTOBER 1, 1968

SAGENDORF: OCTOBER 4, 1968

SAGENDORF: OCTOBER 7, 1968

SAGENDORF: OCTOBER 10, 1968

HOUSE GUEST

SAGENDORF: DECEMBER 17, 1978

SAGENDORF: AUGUST 1, 1971

GRANNY

When Poopdeck Pappy and Li'l Swee'pea joined the cast of THIMBLE THEATRE, Popeye established a permanent home for his expanding family. It was an all-male household, however, lacking feminine charm and conflict. A family needs a woman's strong hand, so in the early sixties Popeye's Granny was added to the clan.

Granny is a tough, strong-willed woman who likes to run a tight ship. She has to be that way. Trying to raise Poopdeck Pappy is like raising two gorillas, ten wildcats and a feverish bull elephant in a mobile home.

The little lady has one outstanding claim to fame. She is, without question, the world's worst cook. Granny has developed·several ways to burn water, and her biscuits have paved many driveways in her neighborhood. The male members of the family permit Granny to cook only one meal a year. On this day, a non-national holiday, the men sneak out to the Rough-House Cafe for their dinner. A crestfallen Granny usually joins them before the meal is over.

Granny's feelings about her grandson's sweety, Olive, are much the same as Pappy's. She wishes Popeye would find a girl with more meat on her bones and less on her nose.

WHERE'D THEY GO? DINNER IS READY!

A CONSIDERATE CHILD

SAGENDORF: MARCH 29, 1970

*Told to go outside
and play catch
with Swee'pea—
Dufus does just that*

DUFUS

Dufus, an eleven-year-old, three-hundred-pound boy, has but one burning ambition in life—he wants to grow up to be just like his Uncle Popeye. He is not really Popeye's nephew, but the son of Pooky Jones, an old family friend. The young giant is almost as powerful as the sailor, but his strength usually gets him into serious trouble.

Dufus is also highly cooperative. If he's told to "Step on it" while carrying a pie for Granny, more than likely he'll place the pie on the floor and do just that.

Introduced in the mid-sixties, Dufus is completely devoted to li'l Swee'pea. Because Swee'pea has the brains, and he the muscles, they make an unbeatable pair of playmates.

Dufus' visits to the Popeye home cause a problem for Granny—fifty peanut butter-and-jelly sandwiches is his average predinner snack, and she spends most of her time in the kitchen—and also for Uncle Popeye, who has to foot the large food bills.

The name Dufus was brought home from Vietnam by my oldest son. Used to describe a slow-witted airman, it is an apt name for Popeye's lovable nephew.

SURE CURE

SEGAR: JANUARY 27, 1935

GEORGE W. GEEZIL

George W. Geezil, the ever-angry and dissatisfied customer of the Rough-House Cafe, was created in the early thirties as a companion character for Wimpy. Each of the THIMBLE THEATRE cast becomes disgusted with Wimpy's persistent mooching, but only Geezil wishes with all his heart to see him dead.

Like most big-mouthed braggarts, Geezil is a pushover—especially for the quiet, subtle con games of the hamburger eater. In the midst of his most explosive outbursts of complaining, he is a sitting duck for a complimentary remark from the object of his tirade. A simple word of praise from Wimpy turns him into a fawning yes man, groveling to hear more wonderful things about himself.

On his rare appearances in the Sunday pages today, Geezil usually stops at the town cemetery in hopes of finding a new tombstone engraved with J. Wellington's name. In his disappointment that Wimpy is still alive, he cuts his visit short and leaves town, mumbling that maybe next time things will be more to his liking.

THE SUPPORTING CAST

SIR POMEROY VAUXHALL, 1955

MR. SQUIZZ, 1943

HOOFNEY, 1930

JABBO, 1929

GLINT GORE, 1930

KING BLOZO, 1931

OSCAR, 1931

GENERAL BUNZO, 1931

CHIZZLEFLINT, 1936

TOAR, 1936

POOKY JONES, 1936

KING CABOOSO, 1938

ROUGH HOUSE, 1932

OLIVE'S GRANNY, 1936

FROGFUZZ, 1938

MARTION, 1938

VILMA, 1936

MARS BEAST, 1938

KID NITRO, 1934

PROFESSOR HOLKUS POLKUS, 1937

EMOK, 1971

GRISTLE, 1943

MR. FINN, 1959

METEOR PERSON, 1965

GERARD, 1961

BIG BAR, 1972

RICH WESTERN DADDY, 1973

OLIVE'S UNCLE OTTO OYL, 1970

PATCHEYE THE PIRATE, 1971

KING OF DUNDER, 1971

SUSAN,

SPY, 1929

CAPTAIN KEEL, 1936

PROFESSOR LENZ, 1935

DOOMSDAY DOLL, 1972

JAMES J. JAB, 1936

QID, 1973

SLAG, 1936

BACK STAGE

THE WORDS

From its earliest days, the American comic strip has influenced the language of the world. Segar's THIMBLE THEATRE added *goon* and *jeep* to the dictionary, and Popeye's peculiar speech has produced such familiar words as: *dorg, sanrich, suspose, forget-me-don'ts* and *space-shoot*. But it is the phrases that have caught the reader's eye. Wimpy's "I'll gladly pay you Tuesday for a hamburger today!" was used as an opening remark in eateries from coast to coast. Popeye's philosophical "I yam what I yam, an' tha's all I yam!" hangs in doctors' offices, where troubled patients can benefit from Popeye's simple but profound philosophy.

beetle bailey by **mort walker**

SARGE!

THERE'S GOING TO BE A BIG INFANTRY SHOW AT THE ARMORY. HERE'S WHAT I WANT YOU TO DO

YES, SIR

SARGE WANTS US TO GET UP A DEMONSTRATION ON PHYSICAL FITNESS FOR THE INFANTRY SHOW

HOW ABOUT JOGGING IN TARZAN SUITS? I HAVE ONE

I'VE GOT A POPEYE MASK

DIET IS THE **MOST** IMPORTANT. WE COULD PARADE AROUND WITH THOSE BIG CARROT BLOWUPS

IT WOULD BE A REAL ATTENTION GRABBER TO DO IT IN THE NUDE

WHAT ABOUT MENTAL HEALTH? IF YOU DON'T GET YOGA IN IT, YOU'RE MISSING THE WHOLE THING!

4-20

CLUE ME IN

BEETLE BAILEY by Mort Walker, April 20, 1975

POPEYE APPEARS IN THE STRANGEST PLACES

Few comic-strip characters have been abducted from their own environment into the midst of another. Popeye might appear to be upset by the flagrant use of his name and person in the competition, but secretly he's extremely proud of his appearance in these wonderful strips. He says, "I yam what I yam, an' they mus' think I yam special!"

BLOW ME DOWN!?! THEY IS DEFLAMIGATIN' ME!

SPLAT!!

YOU MISSED! I TOLD YOU YOU NEEDED MORE PRACTICE!

YOU DON'T WANT EVERYONE TO GO AROUND SAYING, "THERE'S POPNOSE," DO YOU?

SAM'S STRIP by Mort Walker and Jerry Dumas, April 5, 1963

TRY SOME OF THIS SPINACH. IT'LL REALLY DO SOMETHING FOR YOU!

SPINACH? UG!

C'MON... TRY IT!

AW... OKAY.

ANY EFFECT?

YEAH! I HAVE AN EXTRAORDINARY DESIRE TO GO BEAT UP POPEYE!

RUSSELL MYERS

BROOM-HILDA by Russell Myers January 4, 1973

SUNDAY ACTIVITY PANELS

Many of the Sunday pieces allowed space at the top for activity panels. These contained paper dolls, comic stamps, puzzles and all manner of projects for children to cut, paste, color or solve.

THIMBLE THEATRE'S SAPPO feature used a variety of these, and at one time the total SAPPO feature was used for cartoon lessons.

After 1938, Joe Musial (who later wrote and drew THE KATZENJAMMER KIDS) and I produced the activity panels.

SAGENDORF: 1941

SAGENDORF: 1944

SEGAR: 1937

WIGGLE LINE _MOVIE_

CUT OUT ALL OF HEAVY BLACK LINES IN EYES— CUT SLITS ALONG THE FOUR DOTTED LINES—CUT OUT WIGGLE STRIP AND—

LENGTHEN IT BY PASTING BLANK PAPER TO EACH END— THEN PUT IT THROUGH SLITS— PASTE ENDS OF SMALL STRIPS AND STICK OVER TOP AND BOTTOM SLITS—。

SEGAR: 1936

WIMPY'S ZOO'S WHO!

"the SPONGETT"
BETTER KNOWN AS THE "RUB-A-TUB"

SAVE THESE CUT-OUTS!

HE NEVER TAKES A BATH BECAUSE HE HAS WATER ON THE BRAIN

1 PASTE THIS PANEL ON CARD-BOARD
2 CUT IT OUT
3 FOLD ALONG DOTTED LINES

JOE MUSIAL: 1940

FAN MAIL

In the thirties, when people were not yet overentertained and there was more time to write, the quantity of fan mail received by a popular comic-strip artist was sometimes staggering. Readers were truly involved in the daily doings of their favorite strip, and the introduction of a new character or a switch in story line would increase mail by the bagful. Segar handled the impossible problem of providing each fan with a special cartoon by photographically reproducing a drawing such as the one below.

In 1937, the creation of Popeye's Cartoon Club brought in even more fan mail than the introduction of Alice the Goon had produced. Membership cards were coveted by adults as well as young people—including Mort Walker of BEETLE BAILEY renown.

Space was left in the balloon for the fan's name, and Segar would sign the cartoon in the lower-left corner

THE AUTHOR'S FAVORITE DAILY STRIP

This example of Segar's subtle—but not too subtle—humor shows his ability to cram a complete story into one daily strip of six panels. Any reader not familiar with what happened in the last segment could pick up the paper, read the strip and be hooked as a new Popeye fan.

SEGAR: MAY 27, 1937

POPEYE GOES HOLLYWOOD

Popeye's growing popularity as a comic-strip character, together with the increase in quantity and variety of animated cartoons, resulted inevitably in a new matinee idol. In 1932, Fleischer Studios undertook the project of putting the sailor into action on the screen. Their efforts were thoroughly enjoyed by the moviegoing public and are now considered classics in the art of animation.

Sammy Lerner, the famous songwriter, was responsible for Popeye's theme song in the animated movies. He was inspired to write "I'm Popeye the Sailor Man" in less than two hours. For many years he didn't want it known that he was responsible for the song—he wasn't proud of it—but today he willingly accepts credit for his musical creation. Lerner's emphasis in his lyrics on Popeye's spinach-eating gave a tremendous boost to the spinach industry. And now children could see in action the wonderful results when

I'm Popeye the Sailor Man
I'm Popeye the Sailor Man
I'm strong to the "Finich"
'Cause I eats me spinach
I'm Popeye the Sailor Man.
I'm one tough Gazookus
Which hates all Palookas
Wot ain't on the up and square
I biffs 'em and buffs 'em
An' always out-roughs 'em
An' none of 'em gits no-where.
If anyone dasses to risk
My "Fisk" it's "Boff" an'
It's "Wham" un 'erstan'?
So, keep "Good Behavor"
That's your one lifesaver
With Popeye the Sailor Man.

Words and music by Sammy Lerner
Reprinted by permission of Famous Music Corporation

Popeye ate his favorite food.

With the arrival of television, the popularity of Popeye cartoons grew and continues to grow. They are seen in millions of homes, and each new generation's love of the sailor and his friends makes him one of television's best-loved heroes.

Today's Popeye cartoons are produced for CBS-TV by Hanna-Barbera in association with King Features Syndicate. And Paramount Pictures plans to release the full-length musical motion picture, *Popeye*, in the fall of 1980.

A promotion drawing by Segar announces Popeye's debut into movies

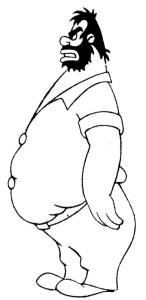

Thimble Theatre characters were simplified for animation

THE FORTIES AND EARLY FIFTIES

The THIMBLE THEATRE newspaper comic strip was produced by a number of men during the late thirties through the mid-fifties. The writing was done largely by Tom Sims, until Ralph Stein took over the dailies in the fifties. Doc Winner, and later Bill Zaboly, were responsible for the artwork. Joe Musial and I produced Popeye-related toys, games, novelties and children's books—and also contributed to the THIMBLE THEATRE Sunday pages.

In 1958, I took over the sole responsibility of writing and drawing the newspaper feature, as well as designing Popyeye products for the syndicate.

TOM SIMS & DOC WINNER: JULY 4, 1939

TOM SIMS & BILL ZABOLY: JUNE 15, 1943

RALPH STEIN & BILL ZABOLY: MARCH 12 1955

TOM SIMS & BILL ZABOLY: JUNE 18, 1944

SAGENDORF: 1940

COLLECTIBLES

Lamp: 1935

Popeye was the first comic-strip character to invade, in an important way, the toy and novelty field. The highly individual characters were easily adapted to a wide variety of merchandise. Early models of these once-inexpensive tin, wooden and paper novelties now carry staggering price tags in antique shops and flea markets.

Puzzles: 1930

Tiddlywinks Golf: 1948

Popeye Jack-in-the-Box: 1961

Whiffle Hen Car Hood Ornament: 1928-29

Jeep Doll (13"): 1937

Kazoo Pipes: 1934-60 (over 12 million sold)

Books: 1934

The Big Little Books: 1937-49

Funny Face Maker:
1947-57

Paint Set: 1930's On

Acrobat:
1930

Wooden Doll (6"): 1930's

Tin Wind-Up Toys: 1932

Bank: 1930's-40's

Balloon
Pump: 1957

Animated Figures:
1950-60's

Jigsaw Puzzle: 1948

Doll (16") and
Hand Puppet: 1950's

Ring Toss Game: 1933 On

COMIC BOOKS

Not since the dime novel has any form of literature captured children and adults as completely as the full-color comics of the forties.

When the print orders for comic books grew to millions for each issue, King Features decided to produce original material for this lucrative market. Popeye was chosen as number one, and for the next twenty-four years I wrote and drew over two hundred comic books and other cartoon books featuring the sailor.

Today, the adventures of Popeye and his friends are carried on, in comic book form, by two extremely talented men. The creative writing is done by Bill Pearson, and cartoonist George Wildman produces the artwork.

KEEPING UP WITH THE TIMES

One of the problems with a comic feature that has run for half a century is keeping it from looking fifty years old. These recent strips from a daily continuity show how Popeye contends with a very up-to-date problem. Li'l Swee'pea has been cloned, and Popeye has to find his "adoptid" son in a batch of a hundred identical babies. Luckily, Eugene the Jeep turns up in time to help the distraught father.

SAGENDORF: JUNE 15, 1978

SAGENDORF: JUNE 16, 1978

SAGENDORF: JUNE 17, 1978

SAGENDORF JUNE 23, 1978

SAGENDORF: JULY 14, 1978

SAGENDORF: JULY 19, 1978

SAGENDORF: JULY 20, 1978

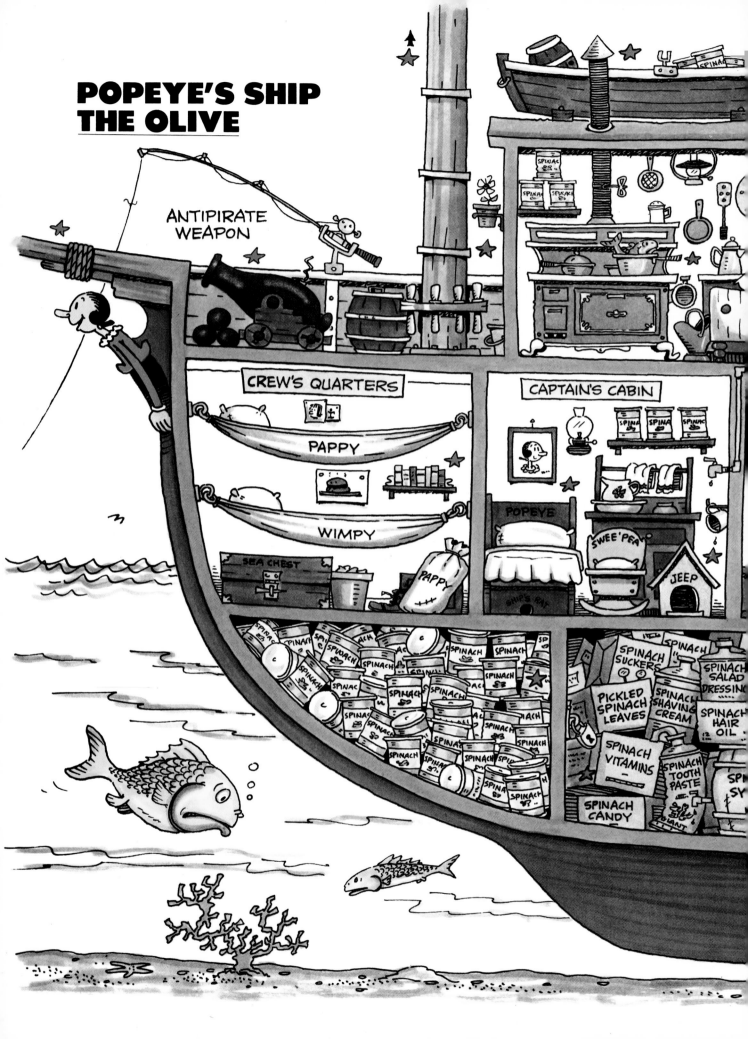

POPEYE AROUND THE WORLD

From his inception, Popeye has enjoyed an ever-increasing international popularity. His belief in right and wrong, his strength, his love for Olive—all are universally understood and enjoyed. Today, in newspapers, books and films—and on television—he is read, seen and heard in nearly twenty languages. In many countries, he is known by other names: in Italy, he is called Iron Arm; in Sweden, Karl Alfred; in Denmark, Skipper Skraek, or "Terror of the Sea."

The six daily strips shown here are all dated September 1, 1978. Popeye's "POW" has the same devastating force no matter what language he speaks.

English

Swedish

French

Japanese

Italian

Greek

THE PAGE THEY ALMOST DIDN'T PRINT

In the thirties, many taboos were placed on the comic artist. The list of don'ts included soiled socks, snakes and too much female showing. Curiously, mistreatment of animals was seldom criticized. Still, Segar was well aware that this page was pushing policy and good taste to the limit. We were surprised when the proofs came back—it meant the strip would be published. Certain that the strip would cause trouble with the public, Segar prepared a letter of apology to send to readers who might complain. After the Sunday comic page appeared, letters did arrive—hundreds of them over the next few years—but none that expressed disapproval. The worrisome page was probably the most popular Wimpy episode Segar created. It certainly received the most complimentary mail.

It wasn't until years later that King Features comic art director, Bradley Kelly, told me what had happened. The page had been passed up the ladder of command until it finally came to rest on the desk of the syndicate's then president, J. V. Connolly. As nervous subordinates watched, Connolly read it and burst out laughing. His only comment was: "It's funny, run it!"

SEGAR: OCTOBER 1, 1933